SARAH LAUGHS

To Judye, who inspires me. —J.J.

To my parents with love. —N.U.

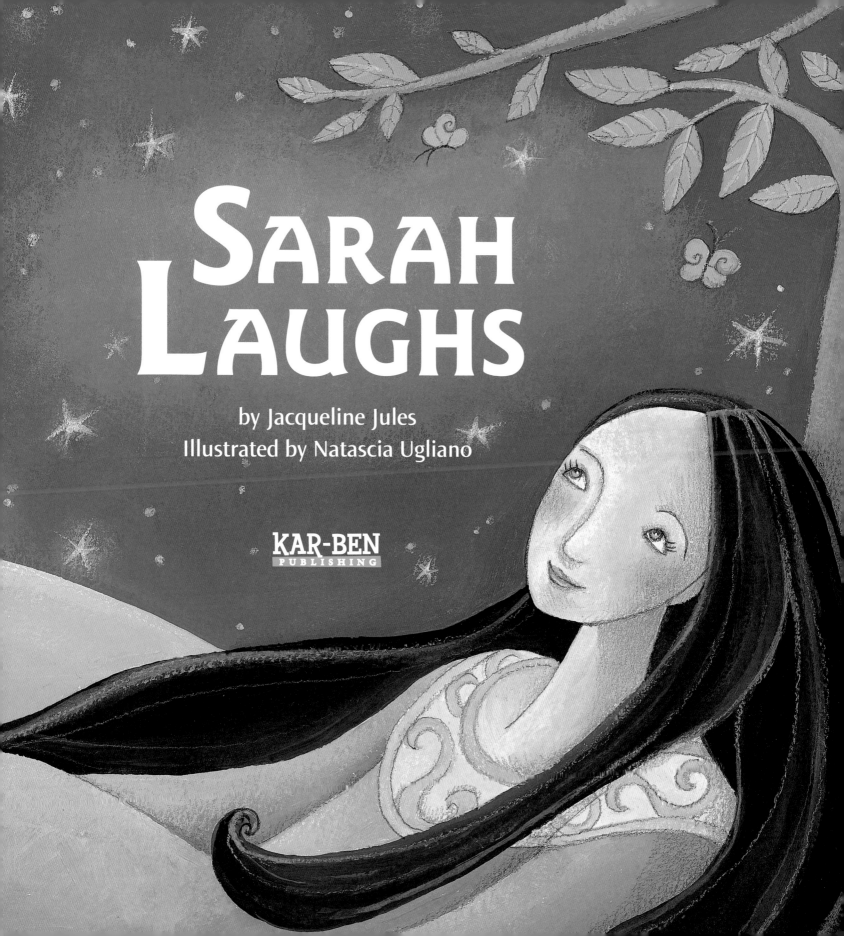

SARAH LAUGHS

by Jacqueline Jules

Illustrated by Natascia Ugliano

KAR-BEN
PUBLISHING

Thousands and thousands of years ago,
a girl named Sarah lived in the city of Ur.
Her name meant "princess," and
she was very beautiful.

When Sarah walked to the well, everyone stopped to stare at the graceful way she carried the urn on her shoulder. Her eyes sparkled like water in the sunshine, and her smile was as warm as a hot drink on a cold night. Legend says that Sarah's laugh made the whole world clap hands with joy.

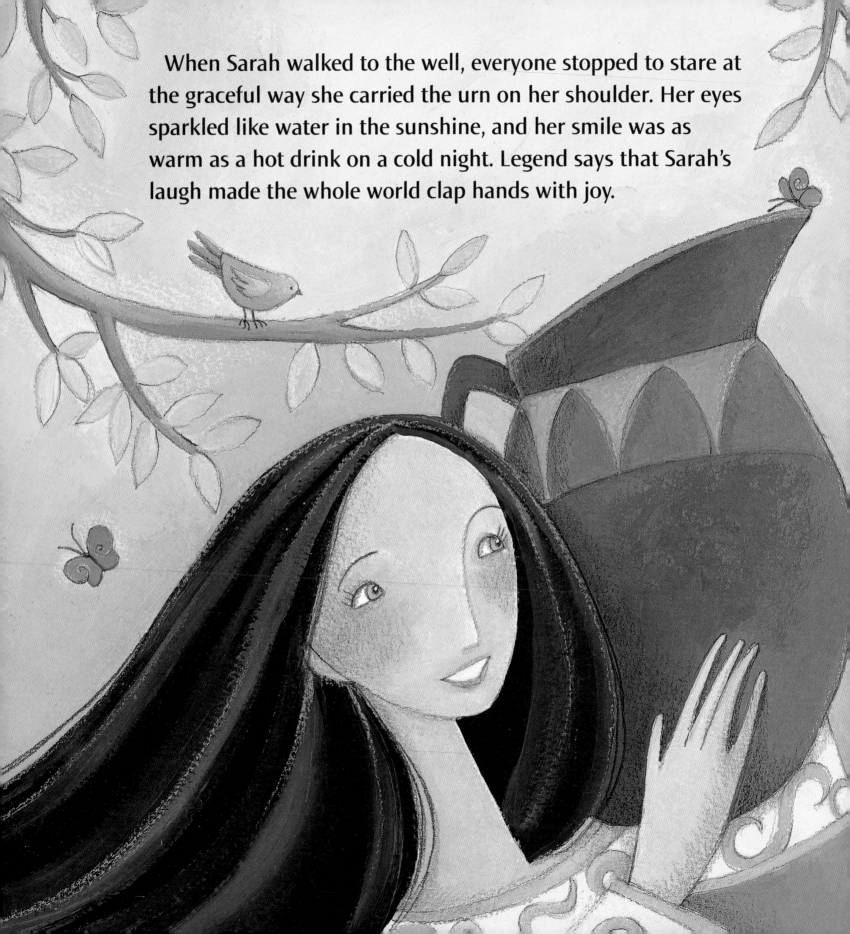

Sarah grew up and married a man named Abraham. Her husband was different from most of the people in their city. Abraham did not pray to idols.

He worshipped one invisible God who was too powerful
to be made into a simple statue of wood or stone.
Together, Abraham and Sarah taught other families
to worship one God, a God who demanded kindness and
good deeds.

One day, Abraham told Sarah he had heard a voice.

"What did it sound like?" she asked.

"Like a bird singing, like the wind in the trees, like every sound in the universe rolled into one."

"What did the voice say?" Sarah asked.

"That we should move to a new place."

Sarah knew this meant they would have to leave their comfortable home. But she also knew Abraham had heard God's voice.

Sarah took a deep breath. "We must go," she said.

Sarah helped Abraham pack their things and gather their animals. Thoughts twirled in her mind like leaves in the wind. "Where are we going? Will we find enough to eat? Will we be safe?" Abraham could not tell her.

"We are following God's voice," he said.

At least they were not alone. Other families came too. At night, they slept in tents. During the day, they walked through the desert with their animals.

They lived as nomads, people who wander from one place to another searching for food and water. Their homes were like bundles of clothes, something they packed up and carried with them.

After traveling for many days, they arrived in Canaan. They camped at Elon Moreh beneath a large tree, forty feet high.

Abraham gazed at the stars through the leaves of this mighty tree, and he heard God's voice again.

"What did you hear?" Sarah asked.

"A promise," Abraham said. "God promised this land to our children."

"But we have no children," Sarah said sadly.

"Not yet," Abraham answered, taking her hand.

Abraham and Sarah continued their journey. They had many adventures, and sometimes they were afraid.

One night, God visited Abraham in a dream and comforted him.

"Count the stars," God said.

"There are too many to count," Abraham answered.

"Exactly," God said. "And one day, the children of your children will be as many as the stars—too many to count."

Abraham told Sarah what God had said. She was so happy, she twirled around and around like a bird ready to take flight. But she did not laugh.

As Sarah and Abraham traveled throughout the land of Canaan, their tent was taken down and put back up many times. But one thing always stayed the same. The doors of Sarah's tent stood wide open, welcoming others to visit and share her food.

People said they could taste a special blessing in the bread she baked. The lamp that glowed inside her tent filled many hearts with joy.

Abraham became a rich man. Sarah never had to worry about having enough. But a sadness still smothered the laughter in her heart.

One night, she held Abraham's hand as they gazed up at the thousands of tiny lights sparkling in the darkness.

"God promised your children's children would be as many as the stars in the sky," Sarah told him. "But I am still not a mother," she said softly. "And we are growing old."

Abraham did not answer her.

"You must take a second wife," Sarah said. "So you can have children."

In those days, many men had more than one wife.
Sarah suggested Hagar, her servant, and Abraham agreed.
They had a son named Ishmael. Sarah thought she would be
happy for Abraham, but it was not the same as having a
baby of her own.

Years passed. Sarah's hair grew gray and lines wrinkled her face. Her bright smile still made the sun wink, but she did not laugh.

Then one hot day, Sarah saw Abraham jump up to greet three strangers. She knew he would offer them food and a place to rest. But she did not know these visitors were really angels who had some important news.

"Sarah," Abraham called. "Please prepare a fine meal."

"It will be a banquet," Sarah promised.

After the meal, the visitors had some surprising
things to say. Sarah listened, hidden from view.
"By this time next year, your wife will have a child,"
the angels told Abraham.

Sarah put her hands on her wrinkled
cheeks. A tinkling sound bubbled from deep
inside her and it skipped through the air.
"I am too old," she laughed. "And my
husband is too old!"

Soon Sarah became pregnant and gave birth to a son. As she held him in her arms, she said, "God has brought me laughter. We will name our baby, Isaac, because it means 'laughter.'"

On the day Isaac was born, the sun
smiled down on Sarah's beaming face.
And the whole world clapped hands
and laughed with her.

Author's Note: The Bible does not describe Sarah or her feelings in any detail. There are many things about her we can only imagine. She is originally called Sarai, but just as God changed her husband Abram's name to Abraham, Sarai's name was changed to Sarah during the course of their story.

I have used *midrash,* (legend) modern biblical commentary, and biblical texts to create a portrait of the matriarch who was a true partner in everything her husband did. My sources include: *Biblical Images* by Adin Steinsaltz, *Etz Hayim Torah and Commentary* edited by David Lieber, *Daughters of Fire* by Fran Manushkin, *Legends of the Bible* by Louis Ginzberg, *Miriam's Well* by Cheryl Bach, *Pentateuch & Haftorahs*, second edition, edited by J.H. Hertz, *Reading the Old Testament* by Lawrence Boadt, *Walking the Bible* by Bruce Feiler, and *Wrestling with Angels* by Naomi Rosenblatt.

Kar-Ben Publishing
A division of Lerner Publishing Group, Inc.
241 First Avenue North
Minneapolis, MN 55401 U.S.A.
1-800-4KARBEN
www.Karben.com

Library of Congress Cataloging-in-Publication Data

Jules, Jacqueline, 1956-
    Sarah Laughs / by Jacqueline Jules ; illustrated by
Natascia Ugliano.
      p.   cm.
    Includes bibliographical references.
    ISBN 978–0–8225–7216–9 (lib. bdg. : alk. paper)
    1. Sarah (Biblical matriarch)—Juvenile literature. 2. Bible
stories, English—O.T. Genesis. I. Ugliano, Natascia. II. Title.
BS580.S25J85 2008
222'.1109505—dc22   2006039738

Manufactured in the United States of America
1 2 3 4 5 6 7–DP–13 12 11 10 09 08